Anna Grossnickle Hines

They Really Like Me!

 Greenwillow Books, New York

For Susan and Ava

Watercolor paints, colored pencils, and a
brown pen were used for the full-color art.
The text type is ITC Usherwood.

Printed in Hong Kong by South China Printing Co.

First Edition   10 9 8 7 6 5 4 3 2 1

Library of Congress Cataloging-in-Publication Data

Hines, Anna Grossnickle.
They really like me!/by Anna Grossnickle Hines.
p.   cm.
Summary: Unenthusiastic about babysitting their brother
Joshua, Abby and Penny play a trick on him, but they
are dismayed when the trick backfires.
ISBN 0-688-07733-1.   ISBN 0-688-07734-X (lib. bdg.)
[1. Brothers and sisters—Fiction.   2. Baby sitters—Fiction.]
I. Title.   PZ7.H572Th 1989
[E]—dc19   87-24211   CIP   AC

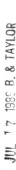

My big sisters are mean.
They won't let me watch
television with them.

Abby takes my toys away from me.

And Penny won't give me any popcorn.

But really . . . they like me.

Mother said, "I'm going to the market. I won't be long. You girls take care of Joshua while I'm gone."

"Okay," Penny said.

"We'll take care of Josh all right," said Abby.

"She means take care of me NICELY!" I said.

"Don't worry, we'll be nice. Won't we, Penny?"

"Sure we will," Penny said. "As long as he's
 nice to us, we'll be nice to him."

"Yikes! Let me out of here!"

"Will you play with me?"

"Not now, Josh," Abby said.   "I'm busy."

"Please play with me, Abby."

"Stop it, Josh!" Abby said. "Go play by yourself."

"You're supposed to take care of me," I said.

"Those are Mother's things! You're going to get
  in trouble!"

"Do you think we should take care
of him now?" Penny asked.
"Yes," said Abby. "I think we should
take care of him REAL GOOD!"

"What shall we do with him?" Abby asked.

"Let's blindfold him," said Penny.

"And carry him far away," said Abby.

"No!" I said. "No!"

"Far away into the woods," Penny said.
"And leave him there!" said Abby. "And
we'll tell Mother he ran away."
"What a good idea!" said Penny.
"No! You can't!" I said. "No!"

"Here we are in the woods," said Abby.

"Yes, this is a good place," said Penny.

"Let's leave him here."

"Good-bye, Josh!" Abby said.

"Look out, Abby! Here comes a bear!"
Abby screamed. "Run, Penny! Run!"
"Help! Help!" I yelled.

"Where's Josh?" Abby asked.

"I don't know," said Penny. "Maybe
 the bear got him."

"No, I mean it, Penny. I can't find him.
 What if he really did run away?"

"Josh! Where are you?"

"Joshua! Josh, if you are hiding, please come
 out."

"Come on, Josh," said Penny.
"We'll play with you now."
"We're sorry, Josh," said Abby.
"We'll NEVER do that
 to you again."

"Do you promise?" I asked.

"Cross my heart," said Abby.

"Me too," said Penny.

Penny gave me a whole pack of gum, and Abby
said we could watch whatever I wanted on
television.

They really like me.